Usborne

My Big HAPPY CHRISTMAS Colouring Book

Illustrated by Jenny Addison

Words by Alice James

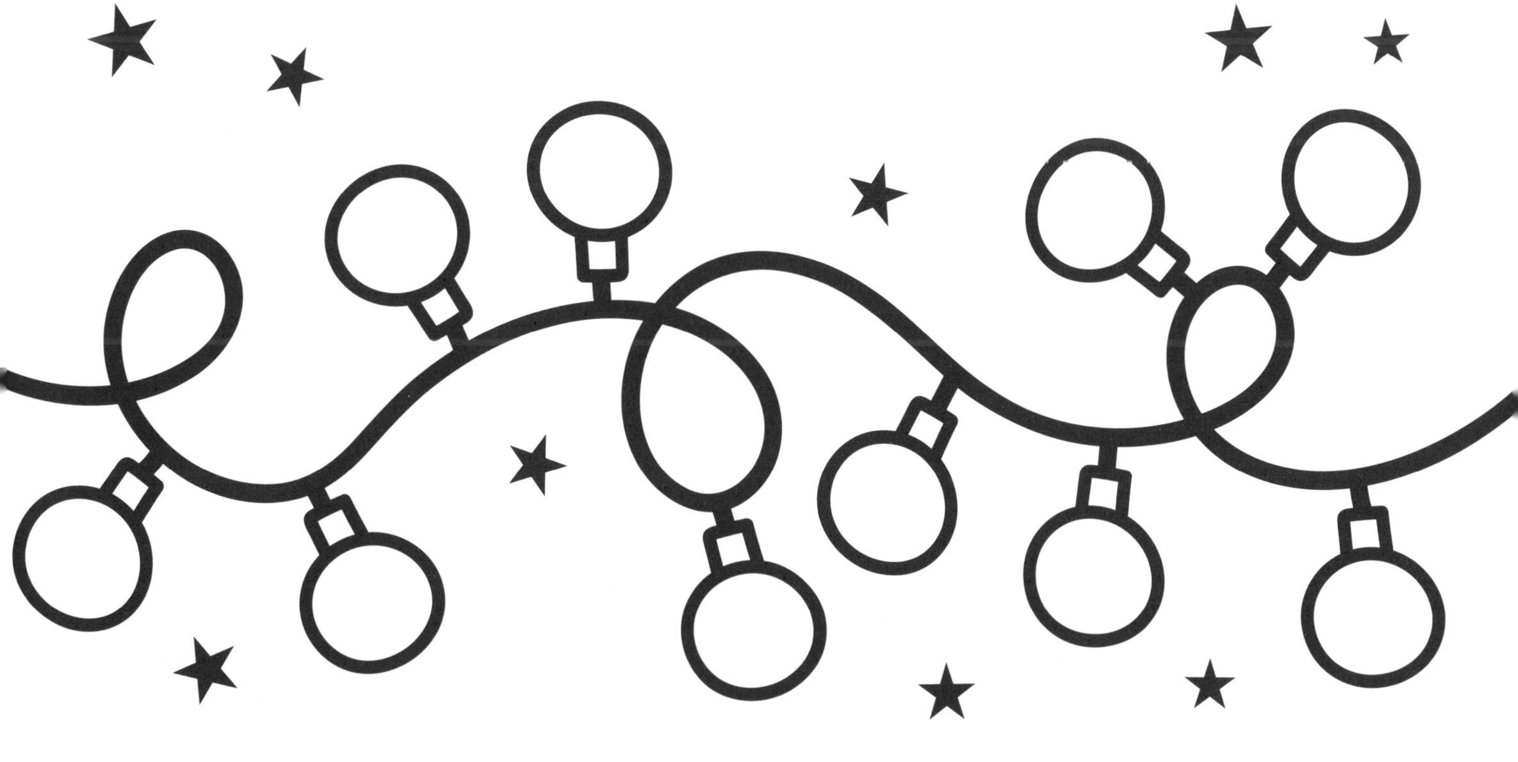

A softly falling snowflake

I'm baking Christmas cookies.

A warm woolly hat...

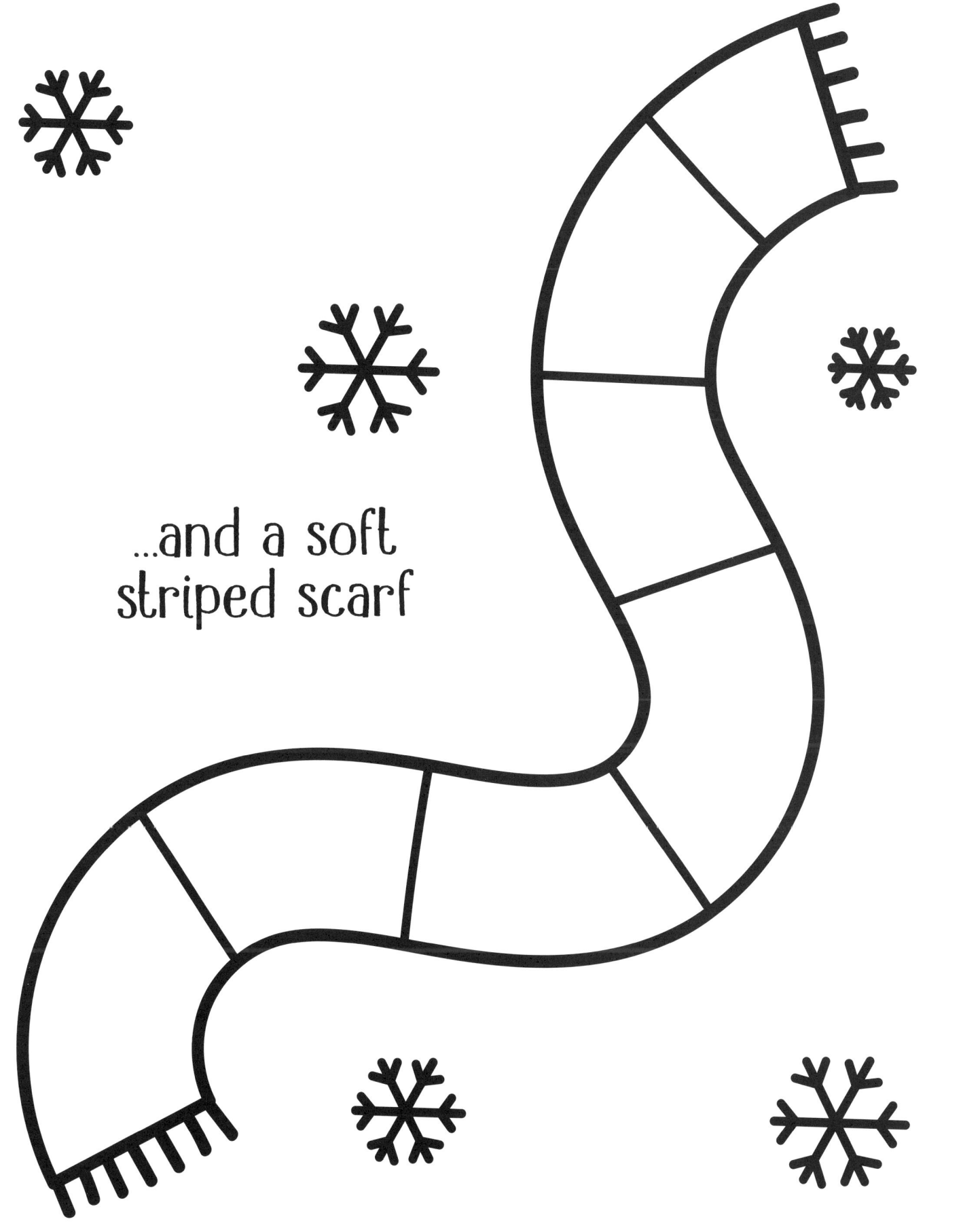

A candy cane

I can grant your Christmas wishes!

I've found the perfect tree.

Sliding through the snow

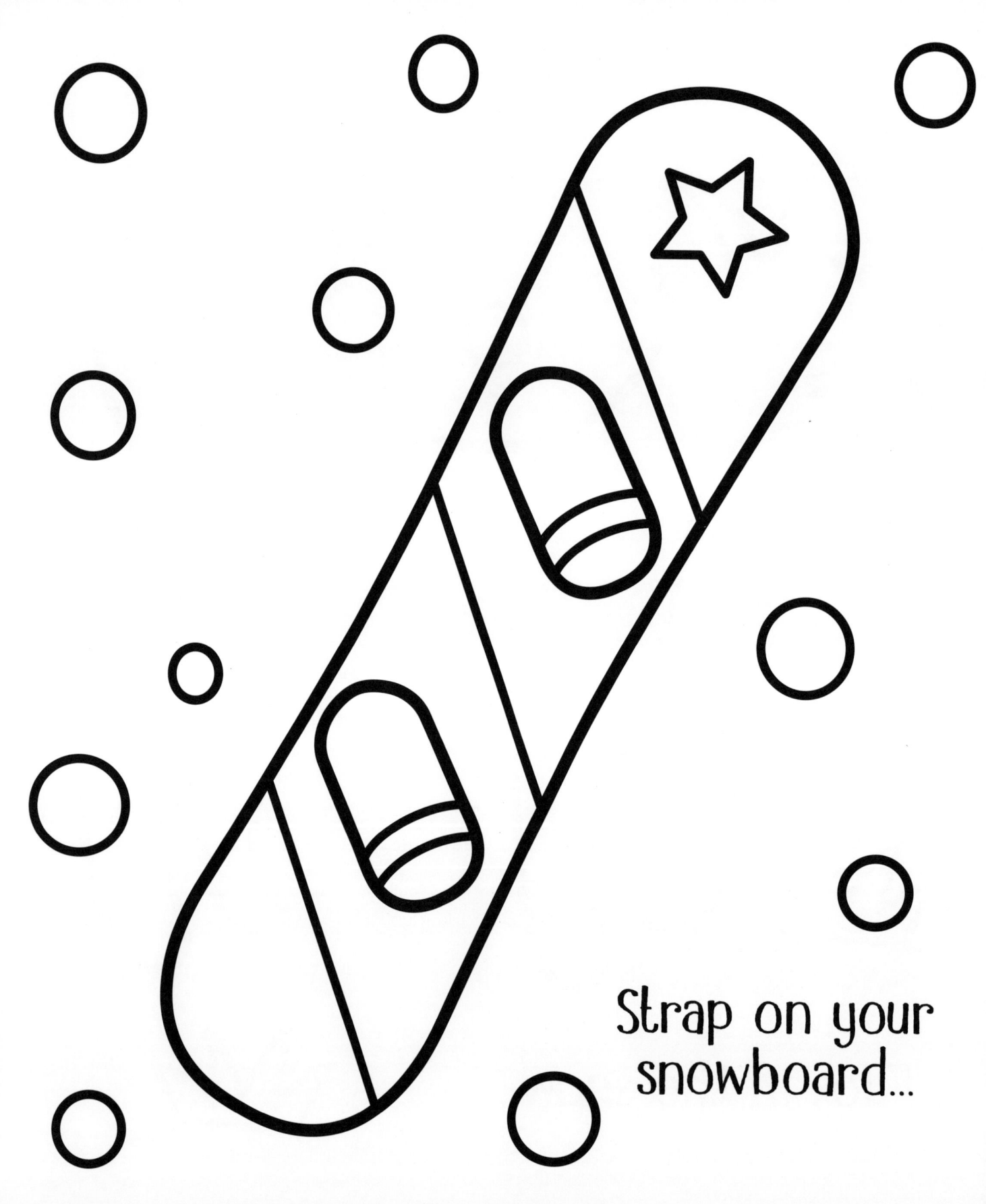

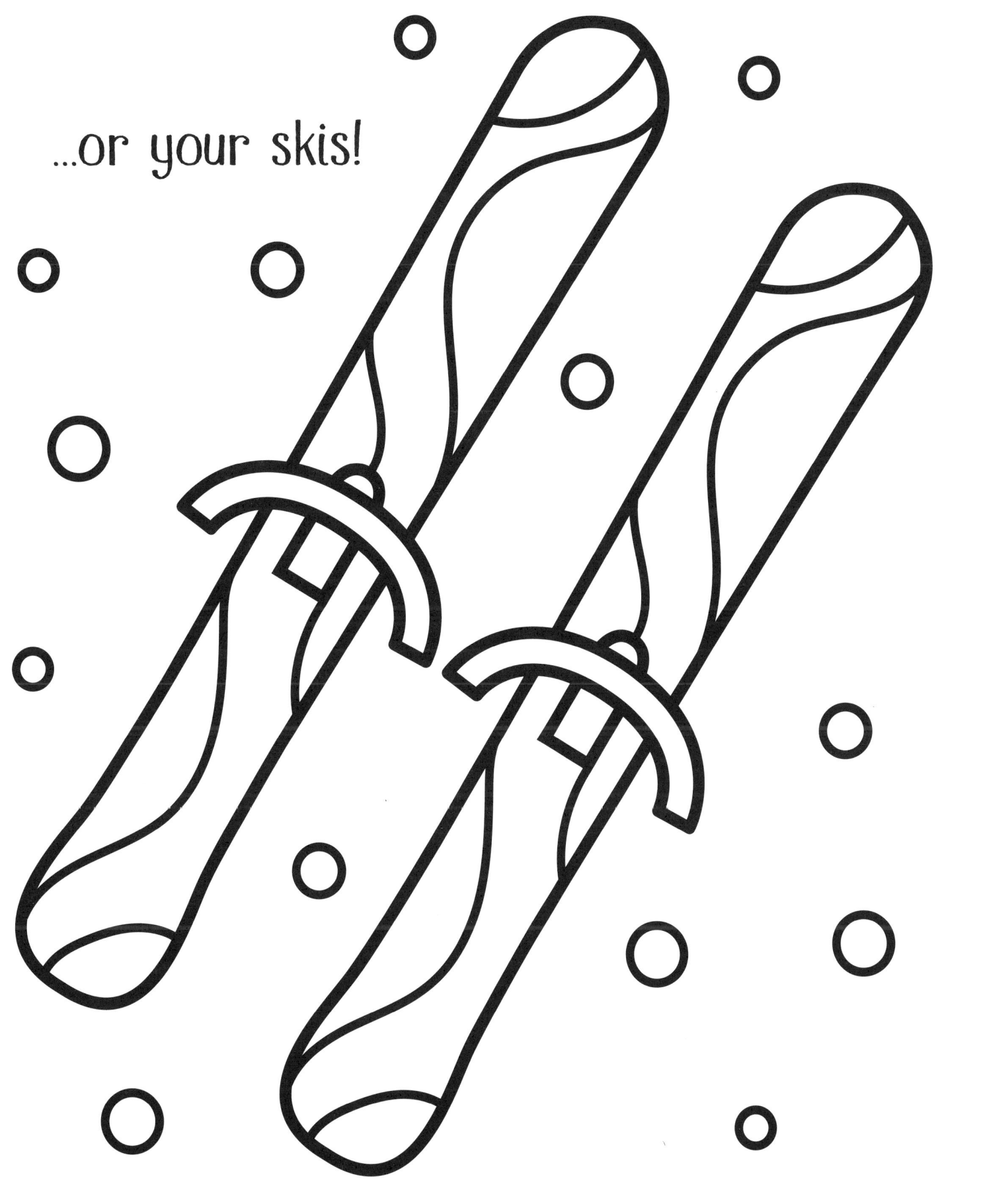

It's snowing!

All aboard!

Squirrel in the snow

I'm a Christmas nutcracker

A lovely warm nest

Listen to the fire crackle.

A yummy yule log...

...and a Christmas cupcake!

Good morning, puffin!

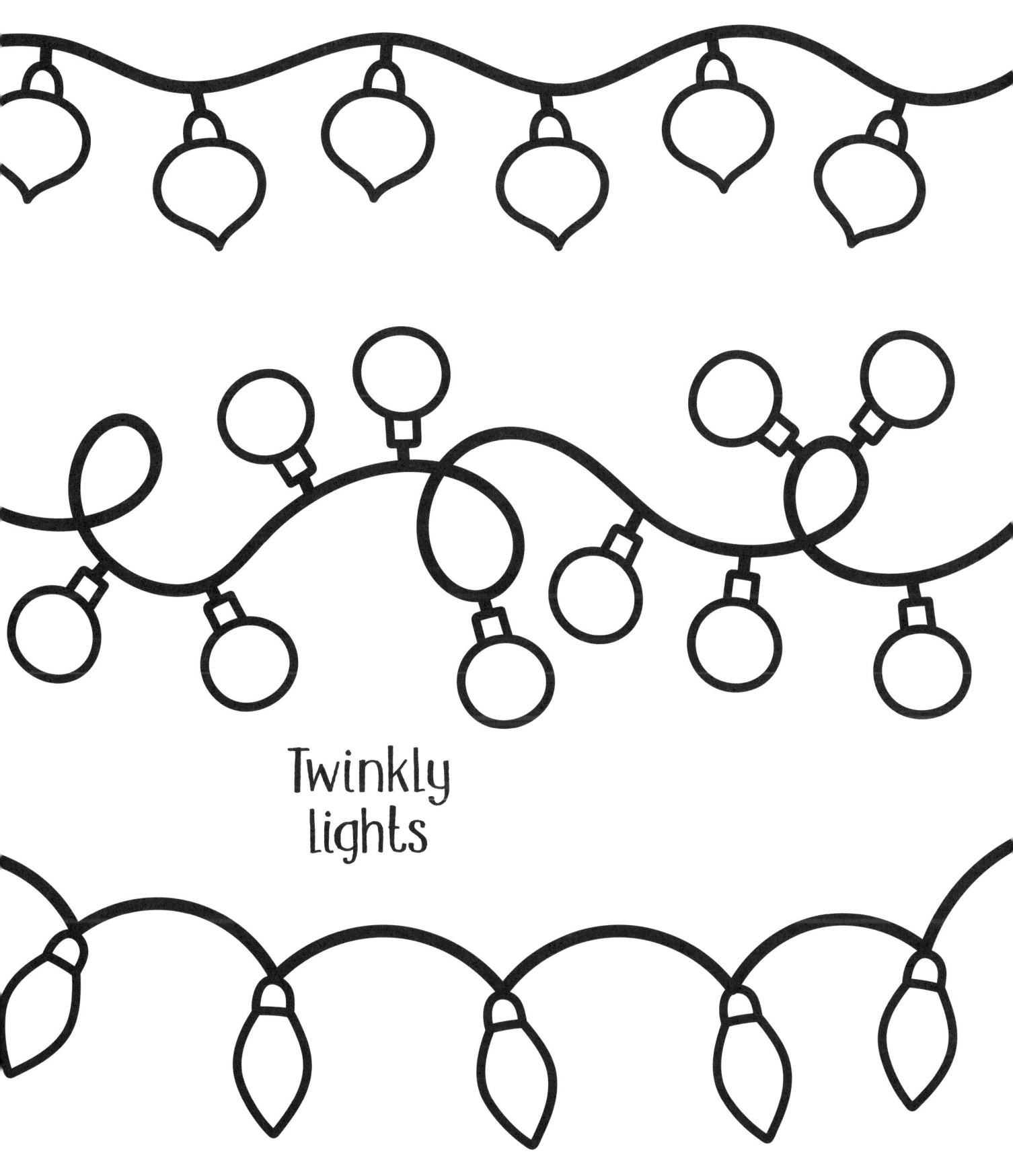

A llama carrying presents!

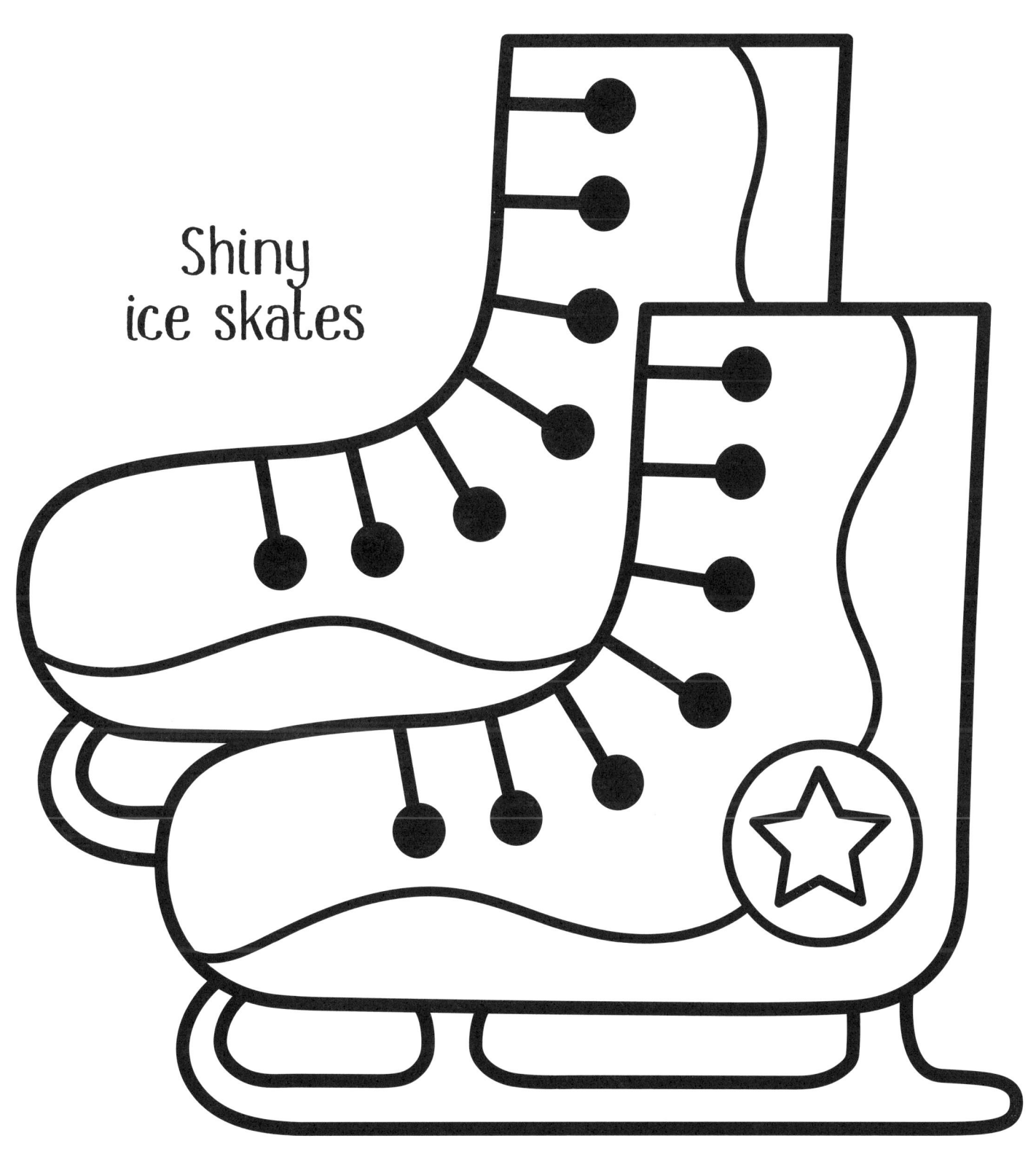

Snowball fight!

A ski chalet

Shoop!

Step inside...

Ding dong, ding dong

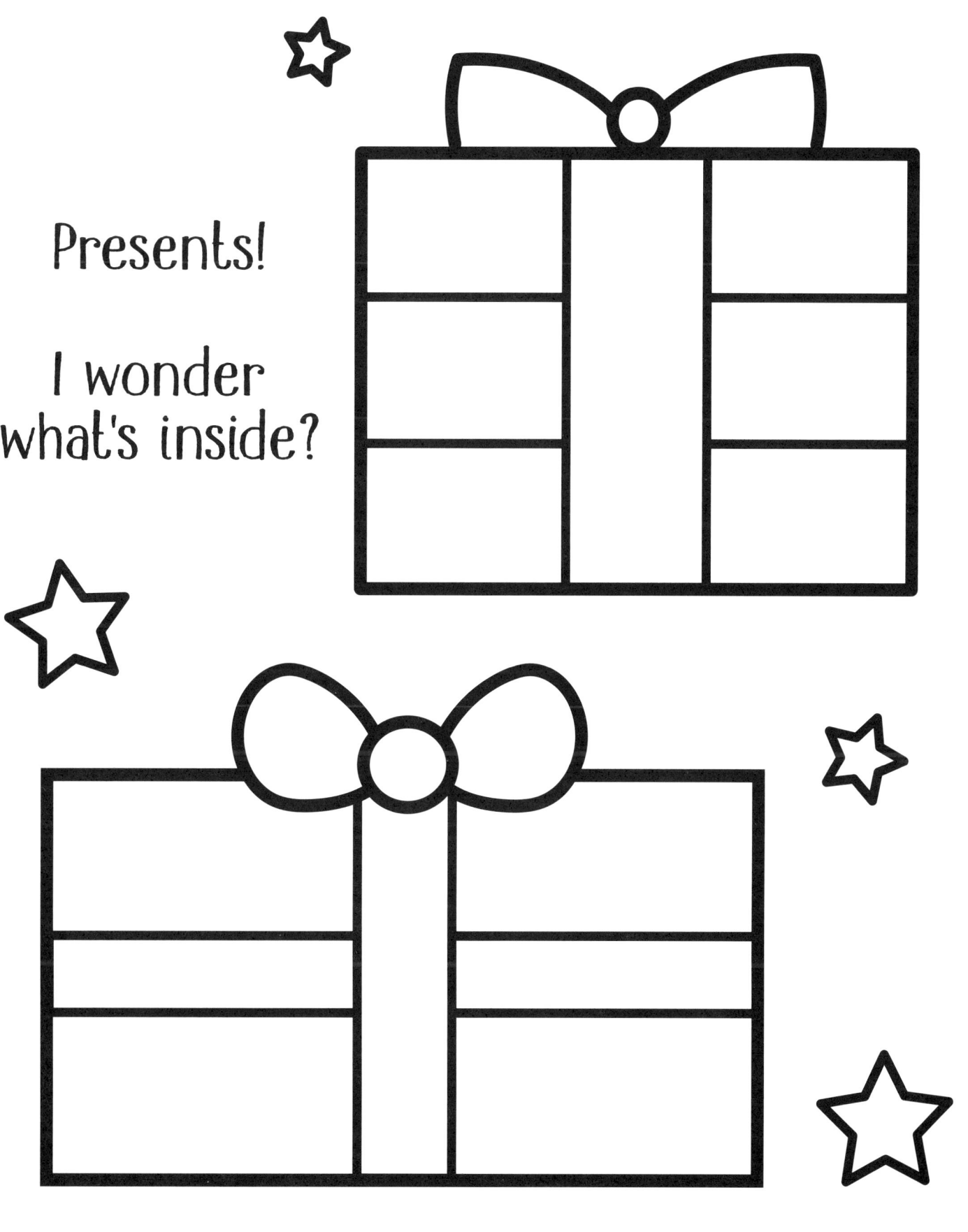